Alien: Doomsday

by

Tony Bradman

Illustrated by Nigel Dobbyn

First published in 2010 in Great Britain by
Barrington Stoke Ltd
18 Walker St, Edinburgh, EH3 7LP

www.barringtonstoke.co.uk

ISBN: 978-1-84299-834-2

Printed in Great Britain by Bell & Bain Ltd

A Note from the Author

I love science fiction and war stories. Best of all are science fiction stories that are about wars – tales of alien invasions and humans who fight back, or battles in space. I thought it would be fun to write a story like that.

So I wrote *Alien*, the first book in this trilogy. *Alien* introduces Jake, a human boy soldier who is part of an endless war. He meets an alien girl, Tala, who ought to be his enemy – but he finds out that she isn't.

Then in the second book, *Alien: Betrayal*, we meet Jake and Tala again. Someone has betrayed them, and for a time they are both in terrible danger.

Alien: Doomsday is the third and final story. Jake and his friends – both alien and human – have to defeat their greatest enemy and save themselves ... and the whole world ...

Contents

Chapter 1

Battle Crazy

Jake was starting to feel very angry. His squad had been pinned down in this area for over an hour, and the enemy still showed no sign of giving in.

He took cover behind some rubble and peered over it. At that very moment, a green laser beam crackled past his head and *ZAPPED* into the wall behind him.

Jake ducked before they could shoot again, but he wasn't scared. *I've lived through a lot of firefights like this*, he thought. *Far too many, in fact ...*

"Tala, where are you?" he said, looking back behind him. His squad was spread out in the rubble around him, firing back with their laser guns. Five human soldiers, five aliens. All of them on the same side now.

"I'm here, Jake ..." said Tala, sliding into position next to him. Tala was a good soldier, and Jake's second in command. But she was also his friend. She stared at him with her golden, alien eyes, waiting for his orders.

She would do anything I tell her, and so would the others, he thought. *Even if it meant they would die. But I can't let that happen. This war has gone on way too long, and too many kids have died. I'd do anything to end it ...*

"I'm going to count to three," Jake said, locking his eyes on hers. "Then I want you and the squad to give me maximum covering fire. Got that?"

"Yes, of course, Jake," said Tala in her soft, lilting voice. She looked worried. "But I don't understand ... What exactly are you going to do?"

"You'll see," said Jake, smiling at her. "Ready? One, two ... *THREE!*"

Then he jumped up and ran towards the enemy, firing his own laser gun from the hip and yelling like a total madman. Seconds later it was all over.

Three enemy soldiers were dead and the rest had chosen to surrender. Jake's squad rounded them up, took away their weapons, and locked them in a cellar.

"What's wrong with you, Jake?" said Tala. She was cross. "You could have been killed! Perhaps you have gone battle crazy at last."

"I can't sit around waiting any more, Tala," said Jake with a shrug. "This stupid war has already taken too much of our lives from us ..."

Just then a soldier ran up. It was Tiny, a member of the first squad that Jake had set up, and the only person Jake trusted as much as Tala. He was very large, very strong and a complete computer geek.

"I think you need to see this, Jake," said Tiny.

Chapter 2

Secret Bunker

Tiny was carrying a laptop. He put it down on a flat piece of rubble and tapped at the keyboard with his big fingers. A picture came up on the screen.

It showed a small, perfect square of concrete in a field of ruins. And set in the middle of the square was something that looked like a steel hatch.

"I've hacked into one of the satellite links that the enemy have set up everywhere," said Tiny. He grinned at Jake and Tala. "I would never have been able to find this otherwise."

"Is that what I think it is?" said Jake, hardly daring to believe it.

"You bet!" said Tiny. "It's got to be the door to the secret bunker! And it's not far

from where we are now – maybe half a kilometre at the most."

"No wonder the enemy have been fighting so hard," Tala said softly. "They knew this is what we have been searching for – the place where all evil comes from ..."

Jake closed his eyes. He tried to hold down the excitement bubbling up inside him. *Could it be true? Have we really found the bunker where The Old Ones and The Elders have been hiding, directing this awful war against us?*

He could barely remember a time without war ... Years ago, aliens called the Krell had come to Earth. At first they lived in peace with the humans they found there. But then they were attacked, and had to fight back to save themselves.

Most of the grown-ups on both sides had been killed. The few adults still alive forced the kids to do the fighting. The Old Ones and The Krell Elders were in charge. They were cruel, and didn't care how many kids died.

Jake had grown to hate the killing. Then he had met Tala, and found out that the Krell kids felt the same. So they had joined forces and formed the United Youth Army. They rebelled against the adults. But The Old Ones and The Elders lost no time in getting together too ...

For a while the fighting had been worse than ever. But over the last few months the kids had pushed back the grown-ups' army. Jake knew that if they could only get into this secret bunker, they might be able to finish the war.

Then I won't have to order human and Krell kids to go off and die ...

"Are you OK, Jake?" said Tala. Jake could hear the worry in her voice.

He opened his eyes and looked at his two best friends in the world.

"I'm just fine, Tala," he said. *"OK ... it's time for us to attack!"*

Chapter 3

Into the Darkness

Jake watched the squad getting ready, the human kids in their combat uniforms, the Krell kids in their cool black outfits, all of them amazing people. *They deserve a better life than this*, Jake thought. *And so do I ...*

"Hold on, Alfie," Tiny said. "You can't take that with you – it's too big."

"What do you mean?" said Alfie. "We might need some real firepower!"

Jake saw that Alfie was carrying a rocket launcher. It was a shoulder-mounted one and his favourite weapon. He was pretty good with it. But Tiny was right.

"Come on, Alfie, use your brains," said Jake. "It's going to be narrow corridors and sealed rooms down there. You could kill us all with that thing."

The rest of the squad had gathered round. They laughed in a nervous way.

"Fair enough," said Alfie, grinning. He put the rocket launcher down beside a rock. "I'll have to rely on you lot and your toy lasers ..."

"We've got plenty of firepower for what we're going to do," said Jake. "Now, it's the usual drill for clearing out a bunker. I'll lead, and we all stay alert, OK?"

Most of the squad just nodded and shrugged. They had cleared plenty of bunkers in their time. But Jake saw Tiny and Tala looking at each other.

"I think I should go in first," said Tiny. "You've done it too often ..."

"And you never know when your luck will run out, Jake," said Tala.

My luck should have run out a long time ago, Jake thought. *Still, it's nice to feel there are people who care if I live or die. But I can't let them do the most dangerous things. I'm Squad Leader – I have to be the one who leads ...*

"No way, Tiny," he said. "You're so big you make an easy target!"

There was more laughter, and even Tiny smiled. But Tala didn't. She was looking grim.

Jake took no notice. "Right then, Tiny," he said. "Blow that hatch!"

Tiny stuck a small device onto the hatch and told everyone to take cover. He tapped at his keyboard, there was a dull *BOOM!* and the hatch flew off.

Jake went over and looked into the hole. The steel rungs of a ladder vanished down into the darkness, and he climbed down. There was a passage at the bottom. At the far end Jake could see a light above a pair of sliding doors.

He carefully headed towards them, the rest of the squad behind him. But suddenly the doors opened with a hiss, and Jake crouched, ready to fire.

"Come in, Jake," said a voice he knew. "We've been expecting you ..."

Chapter 4

Red Lights

Beyond the doors Jake could see a large room. Six people stood inside it, three Old Ones and three Elders. They all wore long golden robes. There was a strange object in front of them, a large black globe that hummed.

Jake kept them covered with his laser gun while the rest of his squad moved into the room and stood in a row beside him. He soon saw The Old Ones and The Elders weren't armed, and that they had no soldiers to protect them.

"Hands up!" he said. "I arrest you in the name of the United Youth Army!"

"You won't be arresting anybody today, Jake," said one of The Old Ones, a woman. She smiled at him. "You'd better put your guns down, all of you."

Jake remembered her now. She had ordered her soldiers – The State Guards, the last adult fighters – to kill him and his squad. But he had got away, and brought Tala and Tiny and his squad out too. They'd been fighting ever since.

"No one move," Jake snapped at his squad. "She can't tell us what to do."

But there's something strange about this, he thought. *Here we are, a squad of hardened kids ready to kill them, and she doesn't seem a bit worried. In fact, none of*

them do. And I don't like the look of that
black globe ...

"Still the same old Jake, eh?" said the
woman. "You're very brave, but you never
listen. But now you've got to. We're going to
offer you a choice."

She put one of her wrinkled hands on the
black globe. The humming grew louder, and
red lights began to wink on and off across its
smooth surface.

"What are you talking about?" said Jake. "And what is that ... thing?"

"Why, it's a bomb, Jake," said the woman. "We decided to make it when we realised you and your friends were about to win the war. We can't allow that."

"Oh, yeah?" said Jake, and laughed. He looked over at Tala and Tiny, but they both looked tense. "Well, one bomb won't help you. It's too late, anyway."

"Ah, but this is a very special bomb," said the woman. "I won't bore you with all the science. Let's just say that if it goes off, then no one will win the war."

"OK, that's it," said Jake, raising his rifle. "I'll count to three. One, two ..."

"Listen to me, Jake," said the woman. "This is a doomsday bomb. Either you give in to us here and now – or we'll blow up the world and everyone in it."

Jake gulped, and an icy chill ran down his spine ...

Chapter 5

Tempting Offer

"But ... you can't mean that!" said Jake. There had been sharp intakes of breath from Tiny and Tala and the rest of the squad. "You'd kill yourselves too."

"That's a price we're willing to pay," said the woman. The other Old Ones and Elders

nodded. *Like a bunch of robots*, thought Jake. "But giving in to us might not be so bad, anyway. We could make your lives so much better."

"Is that right?" said Jake. "Well, I'm listening this time. Tell me how."

Tala and Tiny turned to stare at him, but he kept his eyes on the woman.

"We don't mind admitting that we've made a few mistakes," she said. "But we can change. And you kids have shown just how

brave and clever you are. So we'd find jobs
for you all when we start to build everything
up again. Most of all you, Jake ..."

The woman paused, and for a few seconds
the only sound in the room was the black
globe humming. Jake watched the red lights
blinking on and off.

It was a tempting offer, he thought. *He
could save everyone if he just let the grown-
ups rule the world. He would never have to
use a laser again, never kill anyone or send*

kids to die. He could have a life, maybe even a good one ...

But if they gave in, what had all the pain and suffering been for? Why had so much blood been spilt? It would have been for nothing. And he had a feeling The Old Ones and The Elders would never change, they would always be evil ...

"Do I have to decide now?" said Jake. "I'd like to talk to my squad first."

"No problem, Jake," said the woman. "We can give you a few minutes."

Jake led his squad back outside, into the dark corridor. They stood round him, their eyes fixed on his face. *Whenever I look at them*, he thought, *I see the ones who died – Maria, Wicksy, Shofiq, Katie. I can't let any of them down ...*

"You don't believe them, do you, Jake?" said Tiny. "It must be a trick."

"We'll soon find out," said Jake. "Can you hack into their computer?"

"You bet I can!" said Tiny. He grinned and pulled out his battered laptop once more. His fingers flashed over the keyboard. "What do you want to know?"

"Is there another way out of here?" said Jake. "Maybe a secret staircase?"

"Hang on," said Tiny, tapping away. "There is! And look where it leads."

Jake smiled and shook his head. "I thought so," he said. "That settles it."

Now I know exactly what to do, he thought ...

Chapter 6

Endgame

"Right, Tiny – you're with me," said Jake. "Tala, take the rest of the squad back up to the ground ... and Alfie, make sure you bring your rocket launcher this time."

"Er ... no problem, Jake," said Alfie, puzzled. "But what will my target be?"

"Oh, you'll know it when you see it," said Jake, smiling. "OK, here we go ..."

Tala led the squad down the passage, while Jake and Tiny went back into the room. The Old Ones and The Elders were waiting for them, their faces grim.

"Well?" snapped the woman. "Have you decided? We are tired of waiting."

"Well yes, I have," said Jake. "The truth is that we'd all rather be dead than spend the rest of our lives as your slaves. So set the bomb off if you want."

Tiny glanced at him, surprised. And the woman gave him a very cross look.

"I should have known you'd be brave ... and stupid!" she said. "So be it!"

She pressed the top of the black globe. The humming grew louder and more red lights appeared on it. Jake aimed his laser at The Old Ones and The Elders.

But a door opened behind them before he could fire, and they ran up a staircase.

Jake lowered his laser and turned to his friend. "It's time to show me just how brilliant you are, Tiny," he said. "Can you stop that bomb from going off?"

"I think so," said Tiny. "But I wish you'd told me what you'd planned ..."

"Stop moaning, Tiny!" said Jake, with a grin. "You know you like surprises!"

Tiny shook his head ... and grinned back at him. Jake turned and ran out. He was quite sure in his mind that Tiny would be able to defuse the bomb. Tala and the rest of the squad were waiting for him when he reached the top. Tala opened her mouth to say something – but her voice was drowned by a sudden noise.

They all looked round and saw that a huge hole had opened up in the ground beyond the bunker – and a spaceship was rising from it.

"That's what Tiny found," Jake yelled. "They always had an escape route. What are you waiting for, Alfie? This is the endgame ... take them out!"

Alfie had already grabbed his rocket launcher from the place where he had left it. He took careful aim – and fired. The small explosive rocket WHIZZED through the air – and blew the spaceship to pieces! Jake and Tala and the squad cheered and yelled and punched the air with their fists.

"Is it really over, Jake?" said Tala at last, her golden eyes full of tears.

"Yes, Tala, it is," said Jake. "From now on we're just normal kids again ..."

That might sound boring, he thought. *But I think I'm going to enjoy it ...*

Barrington Stoke would like to thank all its readers for commenting on the manuscript before publication and in particular:

Liam Bailey
Daniel Brown
James Carnall
Susan Dearden
Angus Devine
Sarah Holt
Shane Jones
Aaron McCrossen

Become a Consultant!

Would you like to be a consultant? Ask your parent, carer or teacher to contact us at the email address below – we'd love to hear from them! They can also find out more by visiting our website.

schools@barringtonstoke.co.uk
www.barringtonstoke.co.uk

Have you read the first two ALIEN stories?

**Alien
by
Tony Bradman**

The world is at war!
The aliens are attacking!
Everyone must fight.
But just who is the
enemy?

**Alien: Betrayal
by
Tony Bradman**

Jake has been betrayed.
And it was someone in
his squad.
Can he find out who it
was?

You can order these books directly from our website at
www.barringtonstoke.co.uk

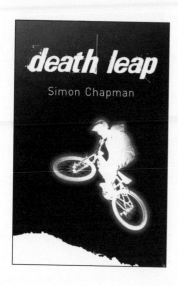

Death Leap
by
Simon Chapman

Jake saw a murder.
The killers saw Jake.
Now the killers are after
him ...

Hero?
by
Pete Johnson

Brad has dumped Luke's
sister.
Now Luke has to fight
Brad.
Will Luke come out of it
a hero?

You can order these books directly from our website at
www.barringtonstoke.co.uk